THE BUTCHER SHOP

Leo's Mark

SIDEWALK

presented by **Paul Fleischman** and **Kevin Hawkes**

C I R C U S

CANDLEWICK PRESS

SEE THE BOR
... THE FLYIN

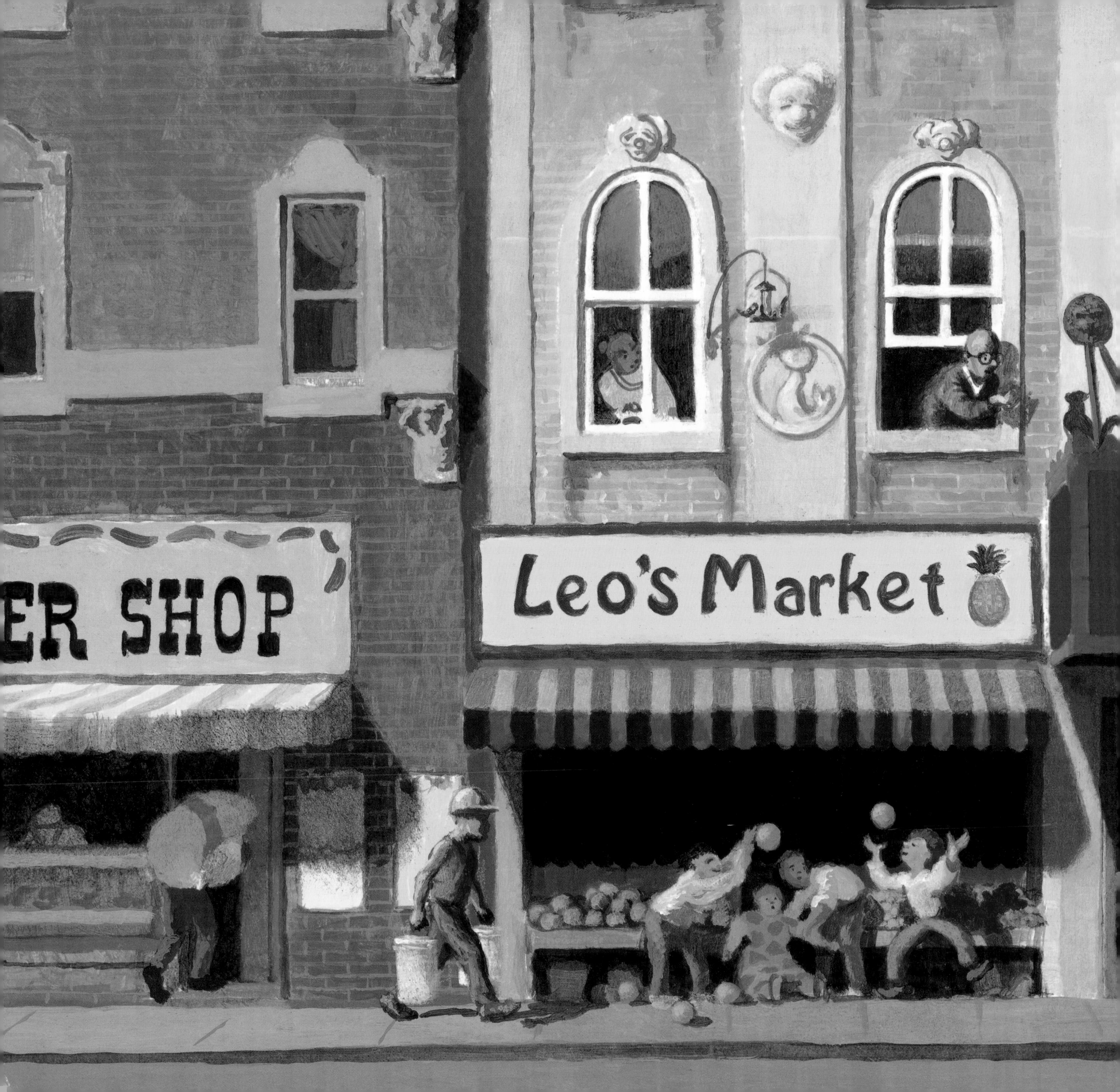
ER SHOP
Leo's Market

GREAT TEBALDI
PRINCE OF TIGHTR

To Ann Stott—K. H.

Story and text copyright © 2004 by Paul Fleischman
Illustrations copyright © 2004 by Kevin Hawkes

First paperback edition 2007

The Library of Congress has cataloged the hardcover edition as follows:

Fleischman, Paul.
Sidewalk circus / Paul Fleischman ; illustrated by Kevin Hawkes. —1st ed.
p.   cm.
Summary: A young girl watches as the activities
across the street from her bus stop become a circus.
ISBN 978-0-7636-1107-1 (hardcover)
[1. City and town life—Fiction. 2. Circus—Fiction. 3. Stories without words.]
I. Hawkes, Kevin, ill. II. Title.
PZ7.F59918 Si 2003
[E]—dc21   2002074168

ISBN 978-0-7636-2795-9 (paperback)

13 14 15 16 17 18 CCP 10 9 8 7 6 5

Printed in Shenzhen, Guangdong, China

The illustrations in this book were done in acrylic.

Candlewick Press
99 Dover Street
Somerville, Massachusetts 02144

visit us at www.candlewick.com

Paul Fleischman is the award-winning author of many books for children and young adults, including *Joyful Noise: Poems for Two Voices*, winner of the Newbery Medal; *Weslandia*, a *School Library Journal* Best Book of the Year and an American Library Association Notable Children's Book; *The Animal Hedge*, illustrated by Bagram Ibatoulline, a *Publishers Weekly* Best Book of the Year; and *The Matchbox Diary*, also illustrated by Bagram Ibatoulline.

"It came out of the blue," he says of *Sidewalk Circus*. "A vision of a ringmaster standing on a city street, describing the sun rising and the clouds changing color as if they were circus acts. Eventually, I decided to leave him out of the story. And then I decided to leave the words out as well." Paul Fleischman lives in Santa Cruz, California.

Kevin Hawkes is the illustrator of a number of popular books for children, including *Weslandia*; *Handel, Who Knew What He Liked*, a recipient of a *Boston Globe–Horn Book* Honor; and *Library Lion*, a *School Library Journal* Best Book of the Year and a *New York Times* Bestseller. He says, "As I worked on *Sidewalk Circus*, I spent a lot of time in Portland, Maine. I was amazed by all the things going on in the city, and all the people and things I had never really noticed before. I am grateful to Paul Fleischman for opening my eyes." Kevin Hawkes lives with his family in Gorham, Maine.